The Sugar Cookie Girl

Written and Illustrated by Kelly Campbell

Once upon a time there was a sweet little old woman and a sweet little old man. They lived together in a cozy little cottage. One Valentine's Day, the little old woman decided to make sugar cookies for the little old man. The little old man was so excited. He loved sugar cookies!

The little old man got the oven ready for his wife as she began to make the dough. The little old woman carefully measured all of the ingredients and mixed them together in a bowl. Next, she rolled out the dough and took out several heart shaped cookie cutters from her cabinets. Each cookie cutter was a different size. There was a small cookie cutter, a medium sized cookie cutter, and a large cookie cutter. She thought it would be nice to use the different cutters to make a Sugar Cookie Girl.

First, she used the large cookie cutter to make the body of the Sugar Cookie Girl. Next, she used the medium sized cookie cutter to make a head for the Sugar Cookie Girl. Then, she used the small cookie cutter to make arms and legs for the Sugar Cookie Girl. After the little old woman placed all of the pieces she had cut out together to form a heart shaped girl, she carefully placed the sugar cookie in the oven to bake.

As the sugar cookie baked the little old woman sat down at the kitchen table to read her very favorite Valentine's Day poem. "Today is the day. It's Valentine's Day..." she read as her husband entered the room.

"What is that wonderful smell?" he asked. The little old woman knew that the cookie was ready. She put on her pink and red oven mittens and carefully took the cookie out of the oven. She placed it on the counter to cool. While the cookie cooled she sat down again to finish her Valentine's Day poem. "The day of sweets and treats…" she read when suddenly, she heard a noise from the counter. It was the Sugar Cookie Girl!

Up popped the Sugar Cookie Girl and straight for the door she ran. "Stop little Sugar Cookie Girl!" cried the little old woman and the little old man. But the Sugar Cookie Girl would not stop! She did not want to be eaten, so as she ran she shouted "Today is the day. It's Valentine's Day. You can't catch me, I'm running away!"

And off she ran. All the way down the drive to the

mailbox. Soon she came to a bird perched on top of

the mailbox.

"You look tasty!" said the bird. "I think I'll have you as a Valentine's Day snack!"

"You'll have to catch me first!" said the Sugar Cookie Girl as she ran away shouting "Today is the day. It's Valentine's Day. You can't catch me, I'm running away!"

Next, the Sugar Cookie Girl came upon a cat walking by the road.

"MEOW" the cat said as his whiskers twitched with delight. "I think I'll pounce on you and eat you as a Valentine's Day snack!"

"You'll have to catch me first." said the Sugar Cookie Girl. And off she ran as she shouted "Today is the day. It's Valentine's Day. You can't catch me, I'm running away!"

The Sugar Cookie Girl ran into the woods nearby. After running for some time, she came to a large pond. At the edge of the pond stood an old sly fox soaking in the afternoon sun and sipping up the clear, cool water. When the fox spotted the Sugar Cookie Girl, his nose inhaled the freshly baked aroma coming from the cookie.

"What are you running from?" asked the sly fox.

"They all want to eat me. I think I need to cross

the pond!"

"You're in luck." the fox said. "I was just about to go for a dip. Climb onto my tail and I'll take you across the pond."

So the Sugar Cookie Girl hopped onto the fox's bushy tail and into the water they plunged.

"The water is cold and it's touching my heart shaped feet!" cried the Sugar Cookie Girl.

"Hop onto my back." said the Fox. The Sugar Cookie Girl did just that.

They swam a little further when, it happened again. "I'm getting wet!" cried the Sugar Cookie Girl!

"Quick, you better hop onto my nose!" said the sly fox.

Just as the Sugar Cookie Girl was about to land on the fox's nose, the sly fox tilted his head back swiftly and gobbled the Sugar Cookie Girl up in one BIG bite! "Today is the day. It's Valentine's Day!" said the Fox. "A perfect day to catch Valentine's Prey!" he said as he licked his lips.

That was the end of the Sugar Cookie Girl!

The end!

www.ingramcontent.com/pod-product-compliance
Lightning Source LLC
Chambersburg PA
CBHW040902120626

46551CB00001B/124